A Moon for Seasons

by Ann Turner
illustrated by Robert Noreika

Macmillan Publishing Company New York
Maxwell Macmillan Canada Toronto
Maxwell Macmillan International New York Oxford Singapore Sydney

WINTER

WINTER MOON

Someone has been polishing
that moon, whirring it
on a grindstone until
it is sickle sharp;
the sky hurts
where the moon touches it.

 Macmillan Publishing Company is part of the Maxwell Communication Group of Companies. Macmillan Publishing Company, 866 Third Avenue, New York, NY 10022. Maxwell Macmillan Canada, Inc., 1200 Eglinton Avenue East, Suite 200, Don Mills, Ontario M3C 3N1. First edition. Printed in the United States of America. The text of this book is set in 14 pt. Palatino. The illustrations are rendered in watercolor. 10 9 8 7 6 5 4 3 2 1

Library of Congress Cataloging-in-Publication Data. Turner, Ann Warren. A moon for seasons / by Ann Turner ; illustrated by Robert Noreika.— 1st ed. p. cm. Summary: A collection of short poems that reflect nature in each season. ISBN 0-02-789513-0 1. Children's poetry, American. 2. Seasons—Juvenile poetry. 3. Nature—Juvenile poetry. [1. Nature—Poetry. 2. Seasons—Poetry. 3. American poetry.] I. Noreika, Robert, ill. II. Title. PS3570.U665M66 1994 811'.54—dc20 92-36857

TASTE SKY

The sky empties
buckets of snow,
feathery as small wings.
I lie on my back and watch
them falling, feel them
falling, and taste sky
on my tongue.

WINTERSPRING

Deep winter,
the sun a thumbprint
on a pale face.
Five birds huddle
on my porch rail,
eyes like black seeds shining,
the only spring,
this snow.

ICE FISHING

Five bright shapes,
a black hole widens
and ripples.
Five lines go deep,
an arm shoots up—
one silver fish!

FOREST TIME

Feathers ray out,
death's sundial
where owl struck noon
on one blue jay.

NIGHT GALE

Back-ended to the wind,
a porcupine mumbles
his bad luck,
caught in the night gale,
his tail a prickly flag.
Mumbling and spitting,
he rasps into the maw
of an old tree stump,
and curls up,
spines to the wind.

EYE

Pond flat as a plate,
grasses sewn shut
by ice needles,
no sign of life
except
in the upside-down
bottom of the pond,
a frog's eye opens
and closes.

SPRING

SPRING MOON

Round as a thumb,
wet as a print
on blurred paper,
the white moon's edges
bleed yellow and pink.

MARCH CLEANING

Wind scours the house,
plucks the roof,
jerks the walls tight,
shakes out the fields
and trees of snow.

CHANGE

Water lips
and eats at frozen sheets,
snow crumbles to sand,
the ice on the pond
buckles and warps,
this great decay—
spring.

MOON GEESE

You pressed the cold
circle against my eye,
I jumped back,
the moon so close
I thought it stuck
to the end of the telescope.

Then a dark fleck showed,
grew darker, longer,
and I shouted at
six geese rowing
across a full moon.

FLASH FIRE

First green at pond's edge,
the sedges, then
cattails,
the tips of grasses
burst into green
faster than fire.

PEEPERS

Under the ragged edges
of last year's leaves,
under the wet mats
of brown oak,
under the moss-stitched cloth
of the forest
the peepers come;
one voice,
two,
one hundred coughing winter
out of their lungs,
singing spring in.

MUD KINGS

Sunlight pierces dark
water, touches mud,
warms the backs of frogs
who rise like kings
from their beds.

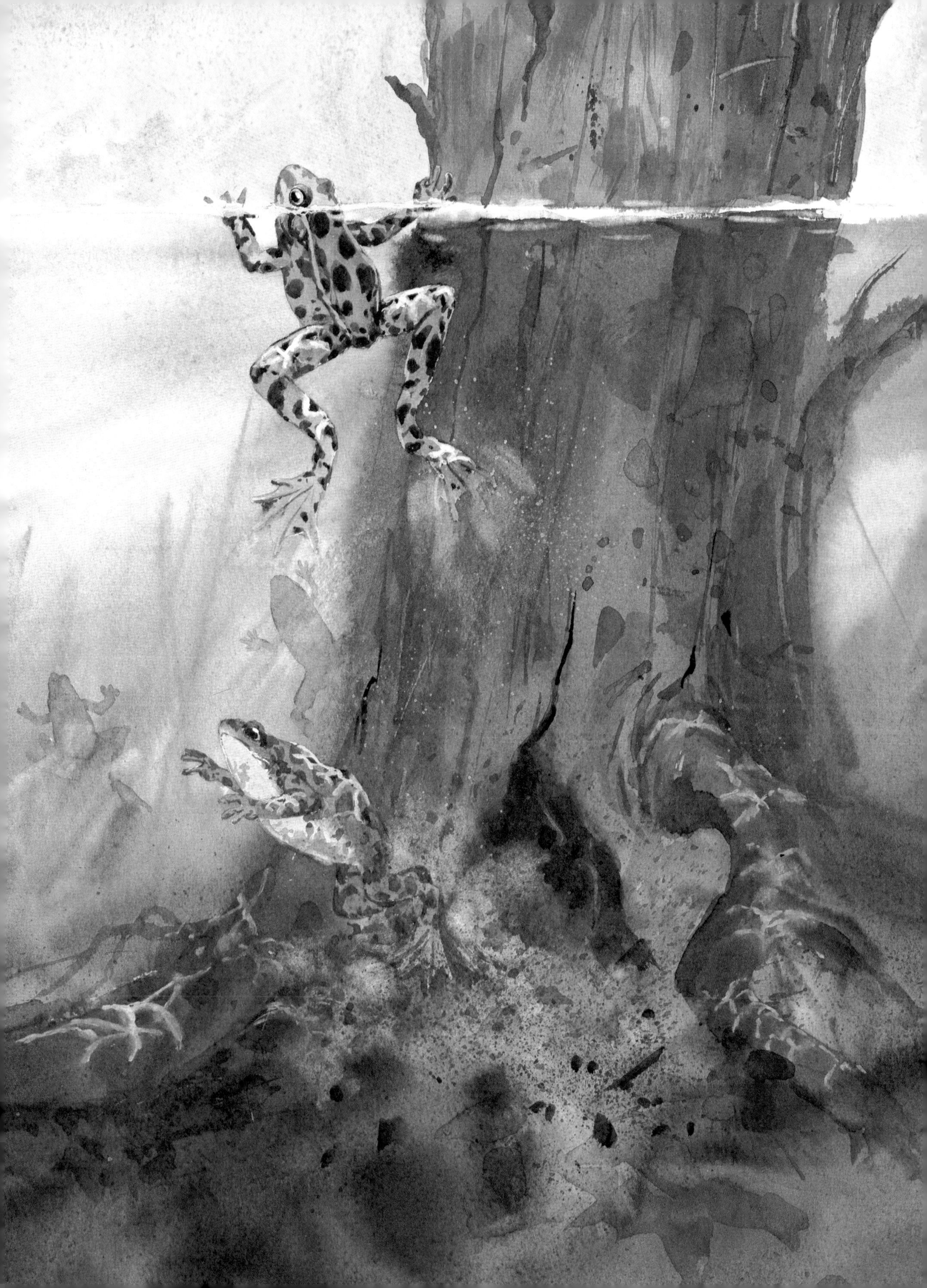

SUMMER

SUMMER MOON

It doesn't stop,
the hurrying, growing,
even after the sun rolls up
the day
and voles sleep, swallows rest,
the moon pours out its light
on crickets, owl, and skunk
while plants stretch up
to that other sun.

ARRIVALS

The swallows light
on sloping wires,
then tails flicking
they slice the clouds
more delicate than surgeons,
let summer in.

STORM

Meadow flowers rub the sky
like kittens nuzzling
a mother's belly;
gold, white, orange
stretch and search until sky
licks them flat again
with its fierce, wet
tongue.

LIGHT WAVES

Here is my sitting rock,
my island under the maple.
Tree shadows wave and splash
on the shore
that is me.

DESSERT

The pond is speckled
with frogs
like a pudding
with too many raisins.
Herons wait like children
eager with their spoons,
plunge and gulp
their pond dessert.

CLEANING

The owl has vacuumed
the wood again,
leaving two gray nubs
of dust again;
bone of shrew, mole, and bat,
rolled in their own
coughed-up fur.

FLAGS

The trees are green and thick
as if summer were here
forever,
and sun and wind and high clouds
were here forever,
except
five bright maple leaves
flag fall.

FALL

FALL MOON

The leaves are down,
the colors gone,
except where the hill
wears the orange moon
like a bright jewel
on its shoulder.

PORCUPINE FEAST

The lump is in my tree
again, eating, moving
stripping the bark,
stuffing the skin of trees
into his spiny pelt.

LANDING

Owl surprised pine,
winging up suddenly
from the dark,
great tufted feet braced
for the branch,
he seized and rocked
and balanced his ever so
soft wings against
the darkness
that holds him up.

BONES

I found them scumbled
in mold, one bone,
two, ribs up
in the forest light
like a fish rising
from the dark.
I took them home
to the beechwood tree
and gave them the blessing
of leaves.

STRAIGHT SOUTH

Herons gone,
folded up their legs,
their head and sword,
full of frog and fish
and careless newt
they fly straight
south,
carrying the pond
with them.

WINTER BED

They're leaving
the pond, the safe
trees, the sweet wind,
crawling back across
the road,
looking for the brown
blanket of the woods,
the soft overhead of leaves,
the hard bed of winter.

WAITING

The frogs lie flat
on the bottom,
brown backs part
of brown mud,
hungry mouths closed tight
on the slow tick
of freezing water,
the sometimes breath,
waiting for sun to warm them
to life.